Gallery Books
*Editor:* Peter Fallon

# THE BOATS ARE HOME

Brendan Kennelly

# The Boats are Home

 Gallery Books

*The Boats Are Home*
was published first in
October 1980.
Reprinted 1983

The Gallery Press
19 Oakdown Road
Dublin 14. Ireland.

© Brendan Kennelly 1980

Cover design by Michael Kane

ISBN   0 904011 08 9 (clothbound)
       0 904011 09 7 (paperback)

Acknowledgements

Acknowledgements are due to the Abbey Theatre, *The Austin Clarke Memorial Broadsheet, Concorde, The Honest Ulsterman, The Irish Times, The Journal of Irish Literature* (Delaware), *Kerry's Eye, The Kildarewoman, Mosaic* (New Delhi), *The New England Review, The Irish Press* (New Irish Writing), *Poems for Shakespeare, Poets and Poetry from Europe 1950-1980* (Louvain), *Profiles 1, The Stony Thursday Book, Trinity Closet Press, The Visitor* (St. Beuno's Press), *Words* (Scotland), *The Writers: A Sense of Ireland* (The O'Brien Press) and to the BBC radio (Scotland) and BBC 2 television.

The Gallery Press receives financial assistance from The Arts Council/An Chomhairle Ealaíon, Ireland.

Contents

*For Bob and Dan*

*To Learn*

There were nine fields between him and the school.
The first field was deep like his father's frown
The second was a nervous pony
The third a thistle with a purple crown
The fourth was a suspicious glance
The fifth rambled like a drinker's talk
The sixth was all wet treachery
The seventh was a man who did too much work
The eighth was downcast eyes, determined to be tame,
The ninth said hello, goodbye.
He thought of the nine fields in turn
As he beat the last ditch and came
In sight of the school on the gravelly rise.
He buckled down to learn.

## The Brightest Of All

The man who told me about the fall
Of the brightest of all the angels
Was Seán McCarthy
Who suffered badly from varicose veins
In the enormous cold classroom.
It wasn't always cold.
On certain days when the sun
Strode like All-Ireland victory into the room
Warming the windows the ceiling the floor
And the chipped desks where the boys
Sat in rows, devoted and docile
As slaves in a Roman galley
Arranged to cope with the sea
And no questions asked,
I thought of the brightest of all
Thrown out of home
Falling, falling
Down through the alien air.
People working the fields
Walking the streets of the cities
That were red circles and squares
On McCarthy's map of the world
Bluegreening a yellow wall
Gaped in wonder at brightness
That darkened the sun to a disc of shame
In the humbled sky.
In this piteous fabulous fall
The brightest of all
Crashed through the crust of the earth
Coming to rest
Deep in its secret heart.
When the scab fell away from the wound of the world
Healed in its own good time
The brightness was trapped in the secret heart
That sustains our birth
Accepts our death
And never complains or praises,
Patient and full of care
As my sister combing her rivery hair.
I was glad that the sun

Was no longer ashamed,
The people no longer dumb
At the sight of a shocking wonder.
And yet I was sad
That the brightest of all
Was trapped
And I thought
One gleam, one single gleam,
Not enough to shame the sun
But enough to brighten a man
May escape from the secret heart
Steal through the cold enormous classroom
Lessen the pain in McCarthy's legs
Where he stood
In the story of brightness expelled
From the painless kingdom
Of an angry God.
But the gleam never appeared.
Seán McCarthy's pain was no lie.
The secret heart is the deepest prison
Under the sky.

## The Stick

The man walked out of the classroom
And strode to the end of the yard
Where the ashtree was in bloom.
It was a calm day, the leaves barely stirred
As he searched the tree for the right strip.
He tried many pieces, threw them aside.
At last, he found the right size and shape
And with his knife sculpted
A thin hard stick, his work of art.
Back in the room, he looked at the boys' faces.
They'd be farmers, labourers, even singers, fiddlers, dancers.
He placed the stick on the mantlepiece above the fire.
His days were listening to boys' voices
Who'd know the stick if they didn't know the answers.

## A Return

The insolence of the dead! With the same black scarf
The worried shirt open at the throat
The forehead high as Shakespeare's
The eyes convinced that every child is a brat
Or parasite, he strides, after more than thirty years,
Into my dream, sits facing me as I sit
Transfixed by the wrestlers stuck in each other.
I feel again a wave of hate
Begin to drown my mind and there
In the struggling arena, I rise, I live,
Amazed at the obscenities scalding my lips,
Untouched when his great head cowers
Then lifts — O God, that unforgettable shape —
Begging the pardon that I will not give.

*The Smell*

The inside of the church absorbed the rain's thunder,
Lightning deceived and killed, the thunder never lied,
The thunder knelt and prayed at the high altar.
I was six years old. I knelt and prayed at her side.

She was a woman in black, she of the white head,
She whose lips rivalled the lips of the rain.
Someone closer to her than anyone had died far back.
That was the story. The story created her pain.

Out of her pain she prayed, always on her knees,
Her lips shaped secrets like rain in August grass.
Her white head, I knew, could not betray or deceive,
The thunder imitated the secrets of her heart.

I knelt at her side, my shoulder brushing her black,
Her lips surrendered visions of her private heaven and hell.
Drugged by her whispers, my head sank into her side,
My body and soul, in that instant, entered her smell,

Not merely the smell of her skin, but the smell
Of her prayers and pain, the smell of her long loss,
The smell of the years that had whitened her head,
That made her whisper to the pallid Christ on his cross,

The rent, dumb Christ, listener at the doors of the heart,
The pummelled Christ, the sea of human pain,
The sated Christ, the drinker of horrors,
The prisoner Christ, dungeoned in flesh and bone.

Her smell opened her locked world,
My closed eyes saw something of mine,
My small world swam in her infinite world
And did not drown but rose where the sun shone

On silence following the thunder's majestic prayer
For all the pain of all the living and dead,
I opened my eyes to the silence
Blessing her black clothes, her white head,

Blessing the smell that had told me something
Beyond lips' whispers and heart's prayer.
She took my hand in her hand, we moved together
Out of the church into the rain-cleaned air.

*Lost*

To crawl away then from the shame or hurt
Or whatever it was
And to hide below the depths in your heart
Was all you could think of
Because the world was not only
Empty of love
But was a vast rat gnawing through concrete
To find your flesh.
So you took to a street
And entered a house
Emptier than yourself,
A raw place
Bleeding with memories
Of dawning and dying days.
And you knew

They'd be out in the roads looking for you
In no time at all,
Looking, looking for you
As though they needed assurance
You'd once existed
Beyond the shadowed edges of their lives,
Their voices calling your name
Falling like light rain
On your hurt or your shame
There in the cold of the old empty house,
Calling your name
To the road and the street and the air,
Calling with echoing care
To come out come back come home
From your sanctuary of dark and cold.
Was it minutes or hours or days
Before you came out?
Child in the light

You were found
And were never the same again.

Moving through each known face
You are often lost in the darkest place

Tasting the loss that is yours
Alone,
Hearing the voices call and cry
Come back come out come home
And you wonder why
Being lost in yourself should stir
This cry in others
Who seem together
Behind the shadowed edges of their lives,
Their own cries slashing the air
As the day dawns, as the day dies.

## The Horse's Head

'Hold the horse's head' the farmer said
To the boy loitering outside the pub.
'If you're willing to hold the horse's head
You'll earn a shilling.'

The boy took the reins, the farmer went inside,
The boy stood near the horse's head.

The horse's head was above the boy's head.
The boy looked up.
The sun attended the horse's head, a crown of light
Blinded the boy's eyes for a moment.

His eyes cleared and he saw the horse's head,
Eyes, ears, mane, wet
Nostrils, brown forehead splashed white,
Nervous lips,
Teeth moving on the bit.

The sun fussed over it.
The boy stared at it.
He reached up and gave the horse's head
A pat.

The horse's head shuddered, pulled on the reins,
Rasping the boy's hands, almost burning the skin,
Drawing blood to attention.
The boy's grip tightened on the reins,
Jerked the horse's head to order.
The boy was not afraid.
He would be master of the horse's head
Made of the sun
In the street outside the pub
Where the farmer stood drinking at the bar.

Daylight said the boy was praying
His head bowed before an altar.
The air itself became the prayer
Unsaid

Shared between the boy
And the horse's head.

The horse's head guarded the boy
Looking down from its great height.
If the boy should stumble
The horse's head would bear him up,
Raise him, as before,
To his human stature.

If he should lay his head against the horse's head —
Peace.

The farmer came out of the pub.
He gave the boy a shilling.
He led the horse away.
The boy stared at the horse.
He felt the reins in his hands
Now easy, now rasping,
And over his head, forever,
The horse's head
Between the earth and the sun.
He put the shilling in his pocket
And walked on.

*The Whispering Blood*

The brown pony lifted its head
And without the smallest taste of the whip
Quickened lightly up to the wood
Looming in its cool secrets
As though it had explored itself
And brought back from its own darkness
Stories older than roots and branches.
The reins tightened in Tom Enright's grip,
Miss Carmody suggested to the child
That he hide for a while under the shawl
Spread green and white across her lap
And covering her feet.
Down he went, one with the new darkness.
          His world
Was trees and leaves becoming voices, all
Whispering like people gathered round a dead
Woman in a brown shroud in a room
Papered with silent bells, circles of girls and boys
Apart and near as the trees in the telling wood
One with the music of hooves on the road.
Miss Carmody lifted the shawl, said 'Come!'
Behind them, the wood resumed its daily face.
The brown pony was back at its favourite pace.
The child listened like a stranger to his whispering blood.

*Ella Cantillon*

The watcher saw her walk the empty street
The crinkled yellow scarf about her head.
Her face had the waxen polish of the dead
And her walk was crooked. She dragged her feet
As though in pain or shame,
Anguished parody of movement. Across
His mind slipped the sweet syllables of her name —
Ella Cantillon. Then he was
Standing about five yards from the stage
In an open field on an August day,
One with that summer crowd entranced
By the slight girl waiting, purely
Poised. The sunlight became homage
When her body married music and she danced.

## The Gift Returned

He was at the front on the right.
He could hear his brothers' breathing.
He could feel Jack's tight
Grip on his right shoulder. She'd said
'My death will teach you brotherhood.
There will be nobody younger, nobody older,
There will be brothers giving my death back
To the living grass.
The earth is crying out for us
And cares nothing for our grief.
When you bear me from this house
Where, on a fine day, from this hill I could see
Five counties and three rivers,
You will be farther from me
And nearer to each other
Then ever before.
All I know of dying
Tells me it is a tearing
Leading to new binding.
Wash my body
Before you give it back'.

Now, returning her to herself, they bore
Her washed corpse across the stony yard
Where she'd worked for seventy years
And he knew, feeling his brother's fingers
Cut for support into his shoulder
As though he were a drowning man,
Her deadweight was the lightest thing imaginable
To bear for a lifetime in his mind,
Making him adore the distance
That was the love between him and his kind.

Two five-bar gates between them and the road,
The people a black muttering sea,
The brothers four moving pillars
Bearing something familiar and incomprehensible
Over the stones
To the place of skulls and bones,

Small crooked roads ahead
Puzzling the hedges,
Supporting the living and dead
With earth's unkillable courtesy.
They shuffled through silent light
Becoming one under the weight
Of what had lived to be returned
To a deeper love
Than any moving man could ever imagine.

Yet it was there in the patient grass,
In her final silence,
In his brothers' breathing,
In the place authentic beyond words
Where the sense of returning
Swallowed the sense of leaving.

## The Names of the Dead are Lightning

'All my old friends are dying'
You say in your letter.
Last night the wind cried

Through the house and the rain
Flailed at the streets and trees.
I thought of your loss

Knowing too well,
If I tried for weeks,
Not a syllable

Would salve your wound.
Tice. Joe. Jackie. Gone.
Father, why does the sound

Of thunder make me seek
The darkest room in the house,
Sit and wait for the blue flick

Of lightning over the walls?
You know how I hate loud voices
But this voice called

As though it would not be denied
From heaven to earth, from earth
To heaven. All night I tried

To decipher its tone of cosmic command
But all I found was your letter
Flickering in my mind

The darkest place I know.
The names of the dead are lightning.
Tice. Jackie. Joe.

*The Bell*

At six o'clock on a summer evening
    Danny Mulvihill rang the bell.
It could be heard out in Lislaughtin
    And down in Carrigafoyle.

The fields heard it and were still
    As Michael Enright's mind
Lulled by a field of wheat
    Goldening the ground.

Under the bridge the river calmed
    Its lifeblood towards the sea;
Touched by the bell the river kept
    Its depth for company.

At the height of the bridge Jack Jones stood alone
    Hearing the two sounds,
Through his blood flowed river and bell
    As through the summer land.

Then beyond the river adventured the bell,
    Beyond the silent man,
It lingered over every weed,
    It entered every stone,

It celebrated its own life,
    Its sense of itself as a friend
To even the midges and the briars,
    It praised its own end

Which, when it came, was hard to tell
    Since there remained on the air
Presences like happy ghosts
    Summoned from near and far.

25

*The Story*

The story was not born with Robbie Cox
Nor with his father
Nor his father's father
But farther back than any could remember.

Cox told the story
Over twelve nights of Christmas.
It was the story
Made Christmas real.
When it was done
The new year was in,
Made authentic by the story.
The old year was dead,
Buried by the story.
The man endured,
Deepened by the story.

When Cox died
The story died.
Nobody had time
To learn the story.
Christmas shrivelled,
The old year was dust,
The new year nothing special,
So much time to be endured.

The people withered.
This withering hardly troubled them.
The story was a dead crow in a wet field,
An abandoned house, a rag on a bush,
A sick whisper in a dying room,
The shaking gash of an old man's mouth
Breaking like burnt paper
Into black ashes the wind scatters,
People fleeing from famine.
Nobody has ever heard of them.
Nobody will ever speak for them.

I know the emptiness
Spread by the story's death.

This emptiness is in the roads
And in the fields,
In men's eyes and children's voices,
In summer nights when stars
Play like rabbits behind Cox's house,
House of the story
That once lived on lips
Like starlings startled from a tree,
Exploding in a sky of revelation,
Deliberate and free.

*The Visitor*

He strutted into the house.

Laughing
He walked over to the woman
Stuck a kiss in her face.

He wore gloves.
He had fur on his coat.
He was the most confident man in the world.
He liked his own wit.

Turning his attention to the children
He patted each one on the head.
They are healthy but a bit shy, he said.
They'll make fine men and women, he said.

The children looked up at him.
He was still laughing.
He was so confident
They could not find the word for it.
He was so elegant
He was more terrifying than the giants of night.

The world
Could only go on its knees before him.
The kissed woman
Was expected to adore him.

It seemed she did.

I'll eat now, he said,
Nothing elaborate, just something simple and quick —
Rashers, eggs, sausages, tomatoes
And a few nice lightly-buttered slices
Of your very own
Home-made brown
Bread.
O you dear woman, can't you see
My tongue is hanging out
For a pot of your delicious tea.

No other woman in this world
Can cook so well for me.
I'm always touched by your modest mastery!

He sat at table like a king.
He ate between bursts of laughter.
He was a great philosopher,
Wise, able to advise,
Solving the world between mouthfuls.
The woman hovered about him.
The children stared at his vital head.
He had robbed them of every word they had.
Please have some more food, the woman said.
He ate, he laughed, he joked,
He knew the world, his plate was clean
As Jack Spratt's in the funny poem,
He was a handsome wolfman,
More gifted than anyone
The woman and children of that house
Had ever seen or known.

He was the storm they listened to at night
Huddled together in bed
He was what laid the woman low
With the killing pain in her head
He was the threat in the high tide
At the back of the house
He was a huge knock on the door
In a moment of peace
He was a hound's neck leaning
Into the kill
He was a hawk of heaven stooping
To fulfil its will
He was the sentence tired writers of gospel
Prayed God to write
He was a black explosion of starlings
Out of a November tree
He was a plan that worked
In a climate of self-delight
He was all the voices
Of the sea.

My time is up, he said,
I must go now.

Taking his coat, gloves, philosophy, laughter, wit,
He prepared to leave.
He kissed the woman again.
He smiled down on the children.
He walked out of the house.
The children looked at each other.
The woman looked at the chair.
The chair was a throne
Bereft of its king, its visitor.

## The Pilgrim

I see a girl climbing the mountain
In a red blouse and blue jeans
Rolled up to the middle of her shinbones,
No shoes on her feet meeting the sharp stones,
Climbing among rocks, a smile on her face
Though her mind may be bleeding from old
And new wounds. In time, she accosts the saint
And in the silence a story is told,
A drop is added to the deepening sea
At the top of the mountain before she
Faces down to the world from that brief height.
Below her, for miles around, the fields
Are graves for sheep that never saw the Spring light
In grass kneeling to receive the bones and skulls.

*Killybegs*

1

We drove across the mountains and the bog,
Magenta hypnotic in the fields.
To our left, a glacial lake black with cold
Dropped like a cracked abandoned shield.
You said, seeing a river, it was old:
The oldest river twists and turns at ease,
A proven legend casually re-told.
A younger river, hungry for the sea,

Cuts through forest, clay and stone.
We watched the crooked meditative path
Sure of its future, glad to be alone.
Most of the time, sunlight is a wraith
In that land, always vanishing. Now
It sprinted through the mountain-range.
There was a change of gods above us. Below,
All the fields dazzled in golden change.


2

Killybegs. Evening. The Pier Bar.
Four old men drinking pints
Turn now and then to stare

At the sea. Up the blue creek
The boats come, rounding the red buoy.
Piratical bands of seagulls croak

Above the foam.
The boats' bellies are heavy with fish.
The sea has given. The boats are home.

In piled boxes, the fish glint.
The sea's secrets
Are hauled towards a shed,

Hungry gulls following,
Cowards all
Till one whips a fish in his beak,

Veers out over the water
Where *Immortelle, Belle Marie*
And *Pursuit* lie at anchor.

The lone gull
Opens his jaws
Swallows the fish whole

Then turning from the pier he
Spreads his wings
For the open sea.

3
Back on the mountain road
The rain pelting.
Hard to see ten yards ahead.

This is a land of loss.
No sign of the river or the black lake.
Only roadside grasses toss and shake.

Even if we could see
There isn't a house for miles.

Suddenly there's a grey heap
In the road.
A mountainy sheep,

Its legs broken. No cry
As it tries to crawl to a ditch
Pushing grotesquely

With its furred back
Neat head
And nervous neck.

We can do nothing. The grey rain
Beats on nothing
But human helplessness and brute pain.

We drive on.
The sheep lies alone with its hurt.
The black clouds hang from the mountain.

*Between Sky and Stone*

Knee-deep in the river the man stood.
Deliberate in everything he did
The few words he said
He seemed unaware of the expectant crowd
On the bank. Shyly the boy moved towards him
Not even a small disturbance in his wake
Till he stood, head bowed, before the man
Who sprinkled water over him and spoke
Words of blessing drifting like riverbirds
Back over the water into the middle of
The people shifting in anticipation
Of a changed boy returning among them,
The air itself charged with tongues of love,
Flood-promise in the heart's desert, touch of a man
In the river standing between sky and stone.

## A Leather Apron

After he cut the lamb's throat
He held it out from him by the hind legs
And let it kick for a minute or so.
Then he laid it on the table
That was hacked and scarred like a few faces
I've glimpsed in streets. Slowly then he drew
The bleeding knife across the leather apron
Covering his belly.

I saw the lamb's blood
Wiped from the knife into the leather,
From the leather through the clothes, through the skin
Until it lived again in every butchering vein.
Unless he absorbed what he killed, I'll never
Tell the gentling touch of the man.

*Beatings*

Hannify lifted the ash butt and struck
Quilter on the head and back.
For a while Quilter took it standing up
But a blow on the neck
Grounded him. Turning over on
His face, his hands clasped the back of his head.
Hannify's anger seemed more than human.
He hit Quilter till he was half-dead.
Quilter got over it though. For six weeks
He slunk like a hurt cur through dark and light,
Licking his wounds till the strength returned.
On May eve Hannify's sheepdog died.
Five cows were poisoned at a stroke.
No sign of Quilter when Hannify's hayshed burned.

*Yes*

I love the word
And hear its long struggle with no
Even in the bird's throat
And the budging crocus.
Some winter's night
I see it flood the faces
Of my friends, ripen their laughter
And plant early flowers in
Their conversation.

You will understand when I say
It is for me a morning word
Though it is older than the sea
And hisses in a way
That may have given
An example
To the serpent itself.
It is this ageless incipience
Whose influence is found
In the first and last pages of books,
In the grim skin of the affirmative battler
And in the voices of women
That constitutes the morning quality
Of yes.

We have all
Thought what it must be like
Never to grow old,
The dreams of our elders have mythic endurance
Though their hearts are stilled
But the only agelessness
Is yes.
I am always beginning to appreciate
The agony from which it is born.
Clues from here and there
Suggest such agony is hard to bear
But is the shaping God
Of the word that we
Sometimes hear, and struggle to be.

*Living Ghosts*

Richard Broderick celebrates
This winter's first and only fall of snow
With a midnight rendering
Of *The Bonny Bunch of Roses O*

And Paddy Dineen is rising
With *On Top of the Old Stone Wall.*
His closed eyes respect the song.
His mind's a festival.

And now *Romona* lights the lips
Of swaying Davy Shea.
In a world of possibilities
This is the only way.

His face a summer morning
When the sun decides to smile
Tom Keane touches enchantment
With *Charming Carrig Isle.*

I've seen men in their innocence
Untroubled by right and wrong.
I close my eyes and see them
Becoming song.

All the songs are living ghosts
And long for a living voice.
O may another fall of snow
Bid Broderick rejoice!

## The Happy Grass

Here, in their final quiet, the singers lie.
True to the dead, to the living true
The grass is growing as it always grew
Drinking every human cry
Like the rain of summer reaching the repose
Of singers long out of sight.
Will we ever know what the grass knows
Flourishing in green wisdom, green delight?

When delusions of communication cease
And we are victims once again
Of rumours the gossip wind is bringing
We'll celebrate the singers in their peace
Because above the graves of men
The happy grass is singing.

*Play*

Picture the old man of seventy years
Rehearsing his death several times a day.
Between rehearsals, he calls the youngsters
To his side. If, in old men, it is possible
To speak of some belief in innocence
This old man has it in his drowsy way.
When he resigns the world for a spell
He does so only when the children promise
On pain of cross their hearts and hope to die
That they will quietly play about the chair
Where he sits staring down at heaven
Somewhere in his mind adrift in sleep.
'Angels of the earth, angels of the air,
All angels love to play about a sleeping man
And when they play, holy is the watch they keep.'

### The Singing Girl Is Easy In Her Skill

The singing girl is easy in her skill.
We are more human than we were before.
We cannot see just now why men should kill

Although it seems we are condemned to spill
The blood responding to the ocean's roar.
The singing girl is easy in her skill.

That light transfiguring the window-sill
Is peace that shyly knocks on every door.
We cannot see just now why men should kill.

This room, this house, this world all seem to fill
With faith in which no human heart is poor.
The singing girl is easy in her skill.

Though days are maimed by many a murderous will
And lovers shudder at what lies in store
We cannot see just now why men should kill.

It's possible we may be happy still,
No living heart can ever ask for more.
We cannot see just now why men should kill.
The singing girl is easy in her skill.

*Entering*

To be locked outside the image
Is to lose the legends
Resonant in the air
When the bells have stopped ringing.
If water soaks into the stone
And sunlight is permitted to caress
The worm and the root
And the feather lodged in the bird's flesh
Contributes to its flight

It is right
To enter the petal and the flame
Live in the singing throat
Mention a buried name
And learn the justice of the skeleton.

Entering,
I know that God is growth
In this garden of death.
I will always love the strangeness
And never be a stranger
In that thought
As I parry the shrivelling demons
And do my failing best
To rest
Among the flowing, growing forms
That open to my will,
Give access to their mercy
And share their skill.

## The Exhibition

A girl hesitates under elm branches
Their shadows linking arms in the grass,
A few cobwebs depend on the logs of winter,
This tranquil cat suggests murderous ways,

A red setter shines across a road
To a child's muddy wellingtons thrown outside a door,
In a room of subdued music a woman
Fingers the gold in her hair

As if wondering whether to go on a spree
And spend every emotional coin
Or stay in that comfortable house
With himself and the children

Oh and a thousand other pictures
Are catalogued in my eyes.
I wanted to congratulate the artist
But he'd taken himself off down the sky

And was nowhere to be found.
Very soon, the show was over for the night.
I was grateful and decided to keep as a souvenir
My invitation printed in letters of light

Glowing more brightly in my head
The deeper my sleep.
My private collection is growing.
The more I give away the more I keep.

*Sculpted From Darkness*

It is one o'clock on a Christmas morning.
The people are passing over the bridge
On their way to scattered homes.
The darkness bears no grudge
Because the people have tasted the god
Who permits himself to be eaten
By the faithful, the militant, the mindless
And the god-forsaken
About whom the god is not mistaken.
The more he is devoured, the more he lives.
He has an appetite for appetite.
He swallows those who eat him
And inspires them to eat.
How sweet is the god's flesh, how sweet!
The bridge bears the weight of the shuffling feet
And no-one bothers to wonder
At the black passion of water
Spelling out its own hunger
Under the bridge, under the mill
With all its small windows
Closed like books everyone has read
And nobody knows.
And the river articulates its hunger
As it bends with the creek
Twisting like need
Over mud, sedge, weed, gravel and rock.

If the god instructed the people
To enter the blackness, drink the river, eat the mud,
They would enter, drink, eat, because mud, river, blackness
Are three words of the god.
Those who eat the god
Digest the god's language
To increase their substance, deepen their shadows.
Now as they shuffle over the bridge
Their hearts beat with a deeper heartbeat,
The fields they move towards are wrapped
About their bodies like wise cloaks,
Roofs of houses are scales tipped
In their favour, the river and its creatures

Flow and thrive for the flowing people
And the eaten god is happy, finding
Himself in blood. If all is ever well

It is well now in the enlarging darkness
For the people contained as planets
In their appointed places
Each one so sure he seems to find delight
In not being able to see
His own or all those other faces
Sculpted from darkness by the selfsame hand
That motions the people home again
Through the familiar, invisible land
Where the long consequences spread like rain.

## It Was No Crushing Terror

It was no crushing terror, it was a quiet style.
Had I been stoned by the encircling soldiers
I might have run mile after crucifying mile
Till I reached the community of farmers
Working their bullish land in the shadow of the hill.
They'd have sheltered me for months, even years.
All the encroaching soldiers did was smile
As if they were allies of mine and yours.
Yours? Yes, you were suddenly there at my side
Your eyes fixed on each horrific smile
Your left hand raised as if to protect your face.
The leader sneered, 'I want you not to be proud,
Go your different ways, be free, that's all'.
Now I can't find you anywhere in this smiling place.

*Local History*

Pens and pencils conspiring on the desk
The red dog waiting to bite anyone
Who ventures near him without a gun
The boy on the bridge sensing the risk
Of growing up, that is, growing away
From games anticipating the game
That even now he is learning to play
With only the ghost of a ghost hovering about him

Erupted from the serious woman's talk —

The man's footsteps near her made no sound
Though he wore Whiteboys' gaiters in his walk
Up the difficult hillside's frosty ground.
Ignoring her well-meant neighbourly call
He vanished through the estate's orchard wall.

*The Big House*

The springtide ebbed, green weed on the shore
Lay like evidence rejected by the sea.
Among the rocky pools a small man strode
Gathering periwinkles in a bag.
Waves reflected a grim sky.
A night of packed dark that would explode
In clawing rain cat-footed
Over the Shannon.

                        His eyes
Had noted all in a few pools. Finishing
His brief harvest, he walked across three fields
To the Big House, a gapped mask, a racked shell.
He climbed the broken steps, entered, flung
The bag on the cracked floor. Nobody near.
He prowled the windy rooms. They served him well.

## That Look

Jack Scanlon heard the scrape at the back door.
The rat was in the yard outside.
He went out front, untied the wire terrier,
Opened the back door, gave the dog his head.
The scraping stopped, no sound for a while,
A tension grew, the snarling started then,
A throaty menace hard and full.
Scanlon stepped into the sun,
Saw the rat cornered near a wall,
The terrier crouched, head down, fangs clean
As knives in the light. Scanlon moved three paces
As if to give command. With a growl
The terrier killed the fear and hate in
The rat's eyes. I've seen that look in people's faces.

*We Are Living*

What is this room
But the moments we have lived in it?
When all due has been paid
To gods of wood and stone
And recognition has been made
Of those who'll breathe here when we are gone.
Does it not take its worth from us
Who made it because we were here?

Your words are the only furniture I can remember.
Your body the book that told me most.
If this room has a ghost
It will be your laughter in the frank dark.
Revealing the world as a room
Loved only for those moments when
We touched the purely human.

I could give water now to thirsty plants,
Dig up the floorboards, the foundation.
Study the worm's confidence,
Challenge his omnipotence
Because my blind eyes have seen through walls
That make safe prisons of the days.

We are living
In ceiling, floor and windows,
We are given to where we have been.
This white door will always open
On what our hands have touched,
Our eyes have seen.

## A Greasy Pole

The life of any ghost is a search for peace.
See a woman laughing, a man making bread,
A soiled newspaper thrown on a chair
Waiting for a tired reader,
You have the life of the dead.

It is an old intensity made new
For you and me
On our way in a boat to Tarbert regatta,
A pillowfight on a greasy pole
Above a chuckling sea

Whose amusement spreads to Asia
Thrown like an old coat across the map
Of the world as though to keep it warm.
Listen to Lynch's yell vanishing into the water.
That's the style, they cry. That man is in form.

If he keeps this up, he'll make a fortune,
A name for himself, a choice of wives.
The years are salty drops on his freckled shoulders.
Above the spectatorial sea, the dead
Are fighting for their lives

And the boats are still arriving at the long
Grey-stoned quay
Discharging those who mingle
With the people shouting welcome on the shore,
Ghosts of you and me.

*Six of One*

1. *The Barbarian*

Applause he craves, music he loves, plus conversation
Plus working lunches plus the idea of progress
To which his days are a studied contribution.
The damned are a vulgar lot and he'll not bless
Them with enlightenment though there are some
To whom he'll show his sweetest disposition,
Even invite into his mind's kingdom
Where wisdom like a golden brooch is seen
Mesmeric as the thought of his own origin.
To accept one's true function is the problem.
Instruct the ignorant; ignorance is a sin.
Civilization being the urge towards self-control
He makes articulate the pitifully dumb,
Dark souls lit with the glow of his own soul.


2. *The Expert*

The area is limited, it is true.
His knowledge of the area is not.
Right from the start, he knew what to do
And how to do it. All the fish he caught
Were salmon of knowledge and not once
Did he burn his thumb although he touched the fire
Of minds zealous as his own. God's a dunce
When the expert pronounces in his sphere
For he has scoured the fecund libraries
Till each one yielded all its special riches.
Prometheus, overworked and undersexed,
Files in his mind the succulent clarities
Knowing, from the ways of pricks and bitches,
Living is a footnote to the authentic text.

3. *The Warriors*

First, the leprechaun, gritty and sincere
Although his fairy rhetoric might spill
Like heaven upon all heads staring here
Till they felt clonked by some cosmic bible;
And then yon moon-faced fat above the beard
Blowing its dust across the helpless stones
Splutters to be heard, and will be heard
By all who see these two as paragons,
Warriors furring from the visionary north
To execute their comprehensive plan,
Improve the shabby towns, re-write the laws,
Assert for good their quintessential worth
Thus re-discovering heroic man
Pregnant with honour in service to The Cause.


4. *The Missionary*

Dear Souls, I am here on behalf of God.
My mind is made of His light.
I'm ready to shred my flesh, shed my blood
Doing His work among you. It
Is clear that all your gods must go
Back into the darkness from which they came.
I tell you all this because I know.
You, your women and children will know the same.
Pray, O my brothers, for humility
And courage to surrender to the true.
Each man is a star, his soul is bright
As anything the heavens have to show.
Heaven's brightness flows to you from me
And on behalf of God I say, that's right.

### 5. *The Convert*

Reason, king of reasons, reigned alone.
There could never be another
Pretender to the throne
Of understanding. Mary, God's mother,
And other sweet begetters of the divine,
Together with all antics of the magic dark
Within the heart, were unquestionably fine
Illusions, especially when seen to work
For simple mortals. And then, one day,
In the broad sun, reason upped and slipped away
Restless, perhaps, for different air and food.
Our reasonable man felt quite distrait
And shocked admiring friends who heard him say
(He meant it too) 'Thank God! Thank God!'


### 6. *The Savage Ego Is a Circus Tent*

The savage ego is a circus tent
Containing the beasties and the people
Clapped together into a violent
Belch in the middle of a field.
Innocent eyes, as ever, widen at the sight
Of brave man swallowing fire;
Daddy is a surge of lost delight
Finding that tigers are what tigers were.
Elephants, snakes, the man on stilts,
Clowns, Fat Woman, mountain of happy lard,
Vivid fliers defying sternest laws
Replace the solid world that melts
Until no heart can ever again grow hard
Nor anything be heard except applause.